D1442606

J
GN
TRA   Transformers: Spotlight #2:
             nightbeat

THE TRANSFORMERS: SPOTLIGHT #2

NIGHTBEAT

WRITTEN BY: SIMON FURMAN

PENCILS AND INKS BY: MO BRIGHT

COLORS BY: JOHN RAUCH

COVER ART BY: MO BRIGHT,
NICK ROCHE, & JAMES RAIZ

LETTERS BY: SULACO STUDIOS

EDITS BY: CHRIS RYALL
& DAN TAYLOR

A lone wolf, ceaselessly questing, searching for answers to problems big and small, his irregular and unconventional logic, combined with a keen, probing intellect, makes him perfect for the toughest, most convoluted investigations. He loves nothing more than a mystery, the bigger the better, and he never, ever gives up once he has the scent. His name...

...IS NIGHTBEAT.

 Licensed by:

Hasbro
Properties
Group

Special thanks to Hasbro's Aaron Archer, Elizabeth Griffin, Amie Lozanski and Richard Zambarano for their invaluable assistance.

Spotlight

VISIT US AT
www.abdopublishing.com

Reinforced library bound edition published in 2008 by Spotlight, a division of the ABDO Publishing Group, 8000 West 78th Street, Edina, Minnesota 55439. Published by agreement with IDW Publishing. www.idwpublishing.com

Library of Congress Cataloging-in-Publication Data

Furman, Simon.
  Nightbeat / written by Simon Furman ; pencils and inks by Mo Bright ; colors by John Rauch ; cover art by Mo Bright ; letters by Sulaco Studios.
    p. cm. -- (The transformers: spotlight)
  ISBN 978-1-59961-476-2
  1. Graphic novels. I. Bright, Mo. II. Rauch, John. III. Title.

PN6727.F87N54 2008
741.5'973--dc22

2007033984

All Spotlight books have reinforced library bindings and are manufactured in the United States of America.

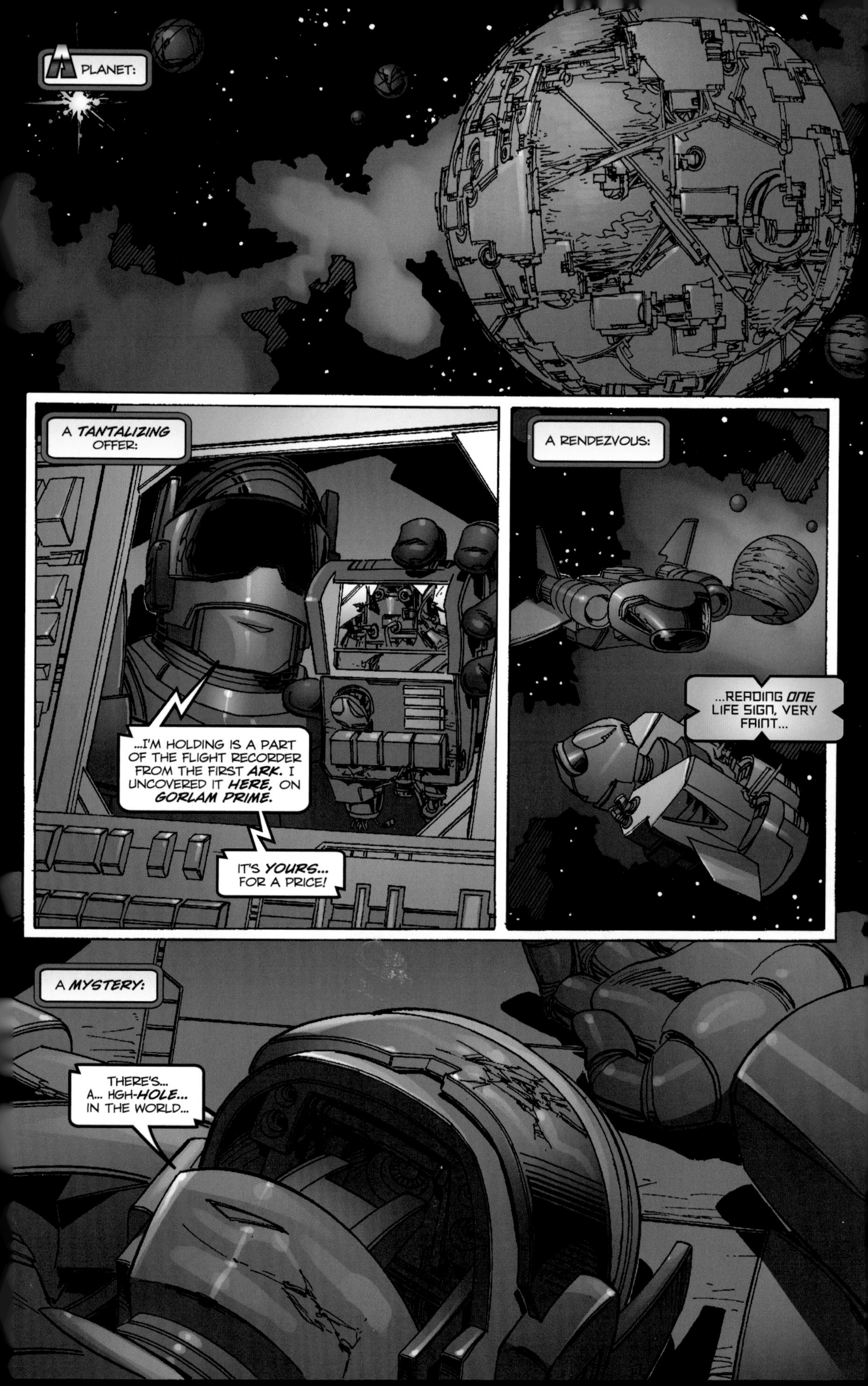

A PLANET:
A TANTALIZING OFFER:
...I'M HOLDING IS A PART OF THE FLIGHT RECORDER FROM THE FIRST ARK. I UNCOVERED IT HERE, ON GORLAM PRIME.
IT'S YOURS... FOR A PRICE!
A RENDEZVOUS:
...READING ONE LIFE SIGN, VERY FAINT...
A MYSTERY:
THERE'S... A... HGH-HOLE... IN THE WORLD...

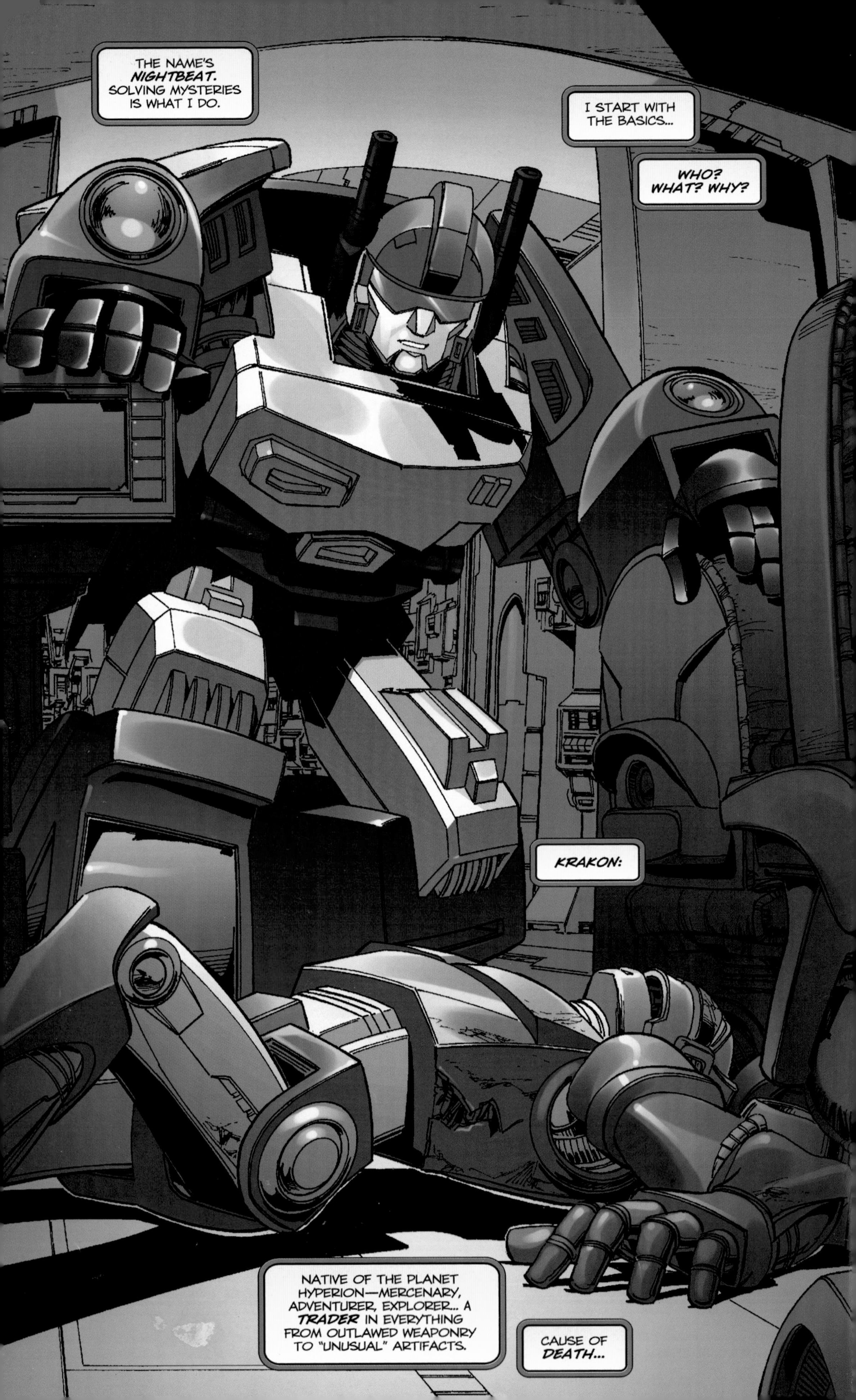
THE NAME'S NIGHTBEAT. SOLVING MYSTERIES IS WHAT I DO.
I START WITH THE BASICS...
WHO? WHAT? WHY?
KRAKON:
NATIVE OF THE PLANET HYPERION—MERCENARY, ADVENTURER, EXPLORER... A TRADER IN EVERYTHING FROM OUTLAWED WEAPONRY TO "UNUSUAL" ARTIFACTS.
CAUSE OF DEATH...

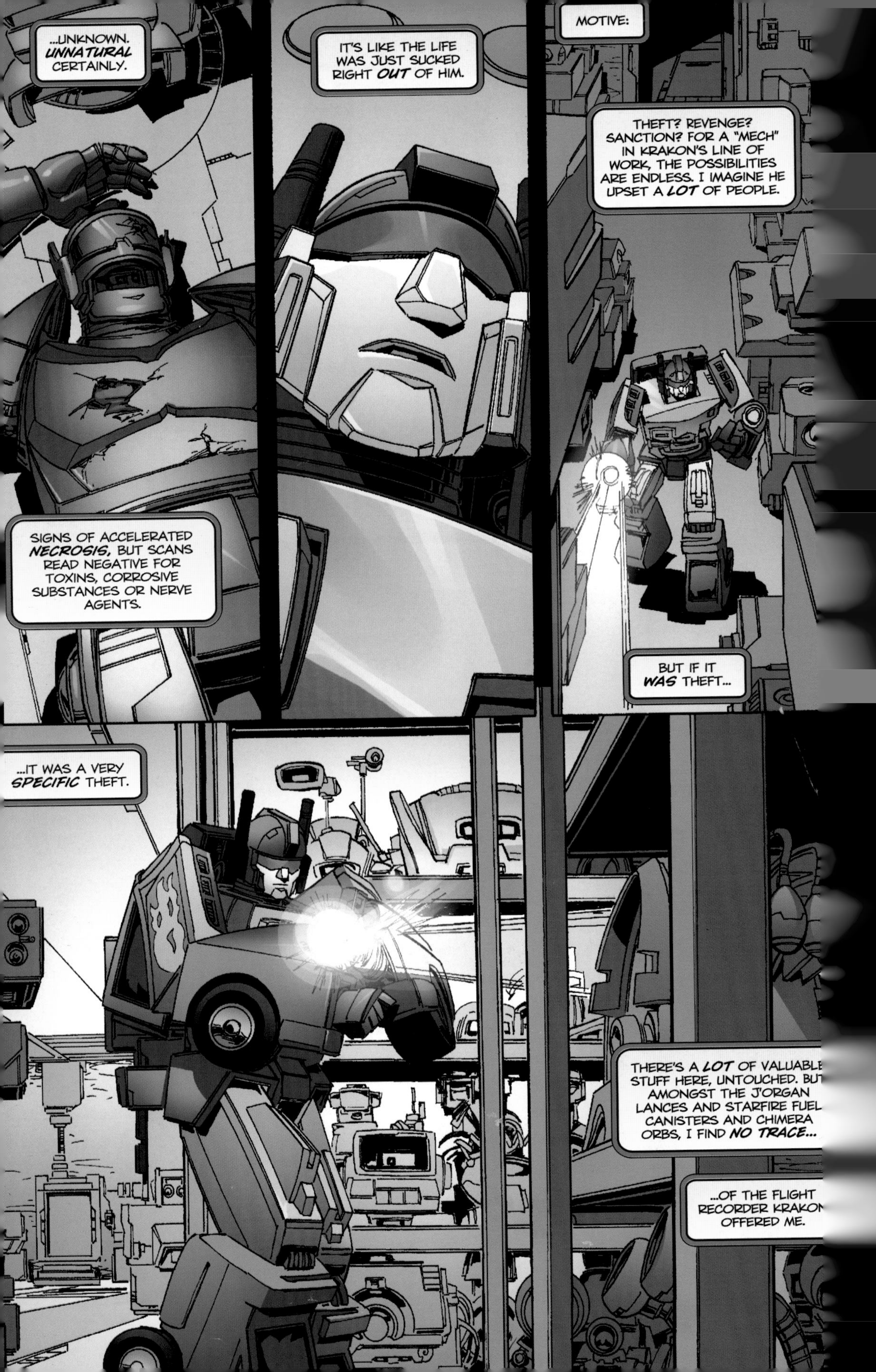
...UNKNOWN. UNNATURAL CERTAINLY.
IT'S LIKE THE LIFE WAS JUST SUCKED RIGHT OUT OF HIM.
MOTIVE:
THEFT? REVENGE? SANCTION? FOR A "MECH" IN KRAKON'S LINE OF WORK, THE POSSIBILITIES ARE ENDLESS. I IMAGINE HE UPSET A LOT OF PEOPLE.
SIGNS OF ACCELERATED NECROSIS, BUT SCANS READ NEGATIVE FOR TOXINS, CORROSIVE SUBSTANCES OR NERVE AGENTS.
BUT IF IT WAS THEFT...
...IT WAS A VERY SPECIFIC THEFT.
THERE'S A LOT OF VALUABLE STUFF HERE, UNTOUCHED. BUT AMONGST THE J'ORGAN LANCES AND STARFIRE FUEL CANISTERS AND CHIMERA ORBS, I FIND NO TRACE...
...OF THE FLIGHT RECORDER KRAKON OFFERED ME.

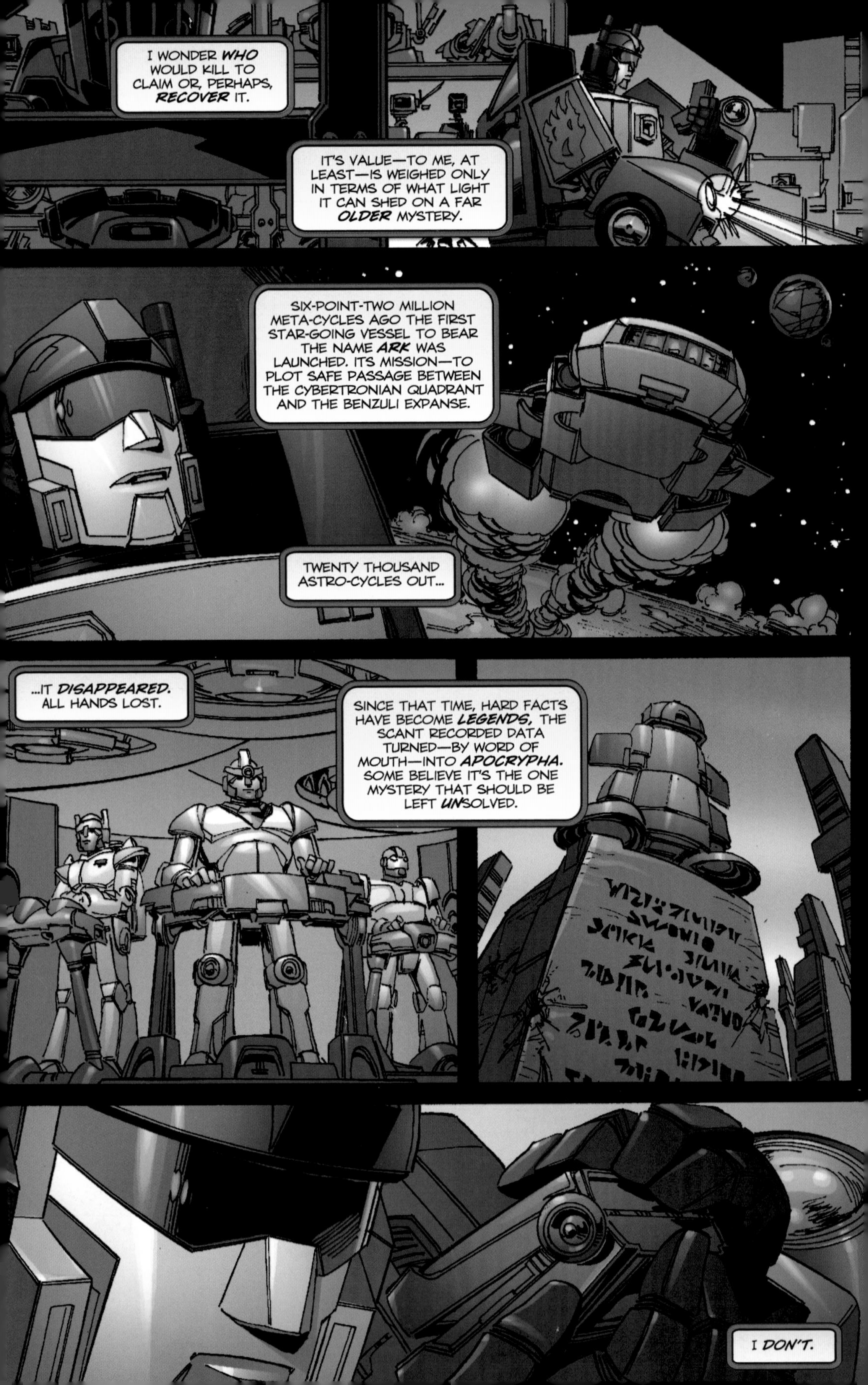

I WONDER WHO WOULD KILL TO CLAIM OR, PERHAPS, RECOVER IT.
IT'S VALUE—TO ME, AT LEAST—IS WEIGHED ONLY IN TERMS OF WHAT LIGHT IT CAN SHED ON A FAR OLDER MYSTERY.
SIX-POINT-TWO MILLION META-CYCLES AGO THE FIRST STAR-GOING VESSEL TO BEAR THE NAME ARK WAS LAUNCHED. ITS MISSION—TO PLOT SAFE PASSAGE BETWEEN THE CYBERTRONIAN QUADRANT AND THE BENZULI EXPANSE.
TWENTY THOUSAND ASTRO-CYCLES OUT...
...IT DISAPPEARED. ALL HANDS LOST.
SINCE THAT TIME, HARD FACTS HAVE BECOME LEGENDS, THE SCANT RECORDED DATA TURNED—BY WORD OF MOUTH—INTO APOCRYPHA. SOME BELIEVE IT'S THE ONE MYSTERY THAT SHOULD BE LEFT UNSOLVED.
I DON'T.

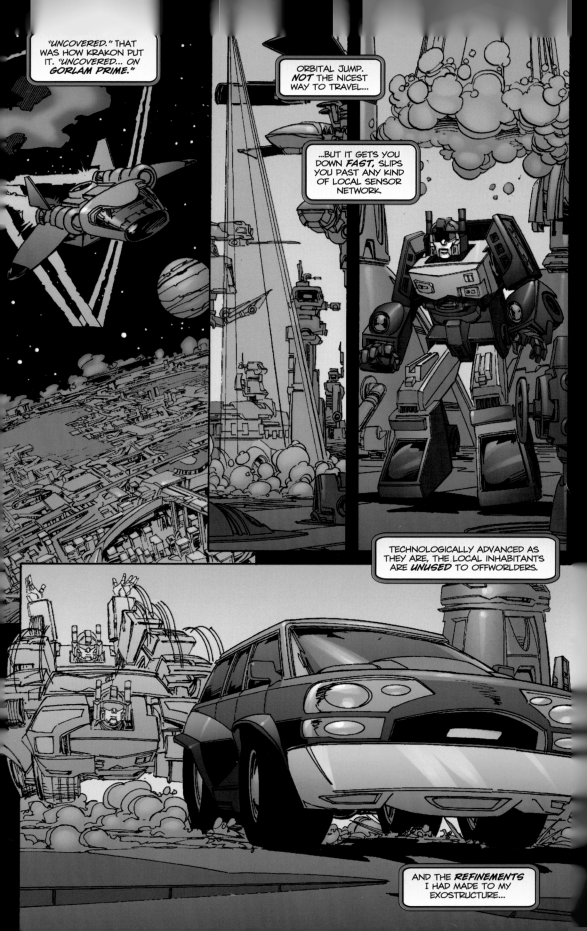

"UNCOVERED." THAT WAS HOW KRAKON PUT IT. "UNCOVERED... ON *GORLAM PRIME.*"

ORBITAL JUMP. *NOT* THE NICEST WAY TO TRAVEL...

...BUT IT GETS YOU DOWN *FAST,* SLIPS YOU PAST ANY KIND OF LOCAL SENSOR NETWORK.

TECHNOLOGICALLY ADVANCED AS THEY ARE, THE LOCAL INHABITANTS ARE *UNUSED* TO OFFWORLDERS.

AND THE *REFINEMENTS* I HAD MADE TO MY EXOSTRUCTURE...

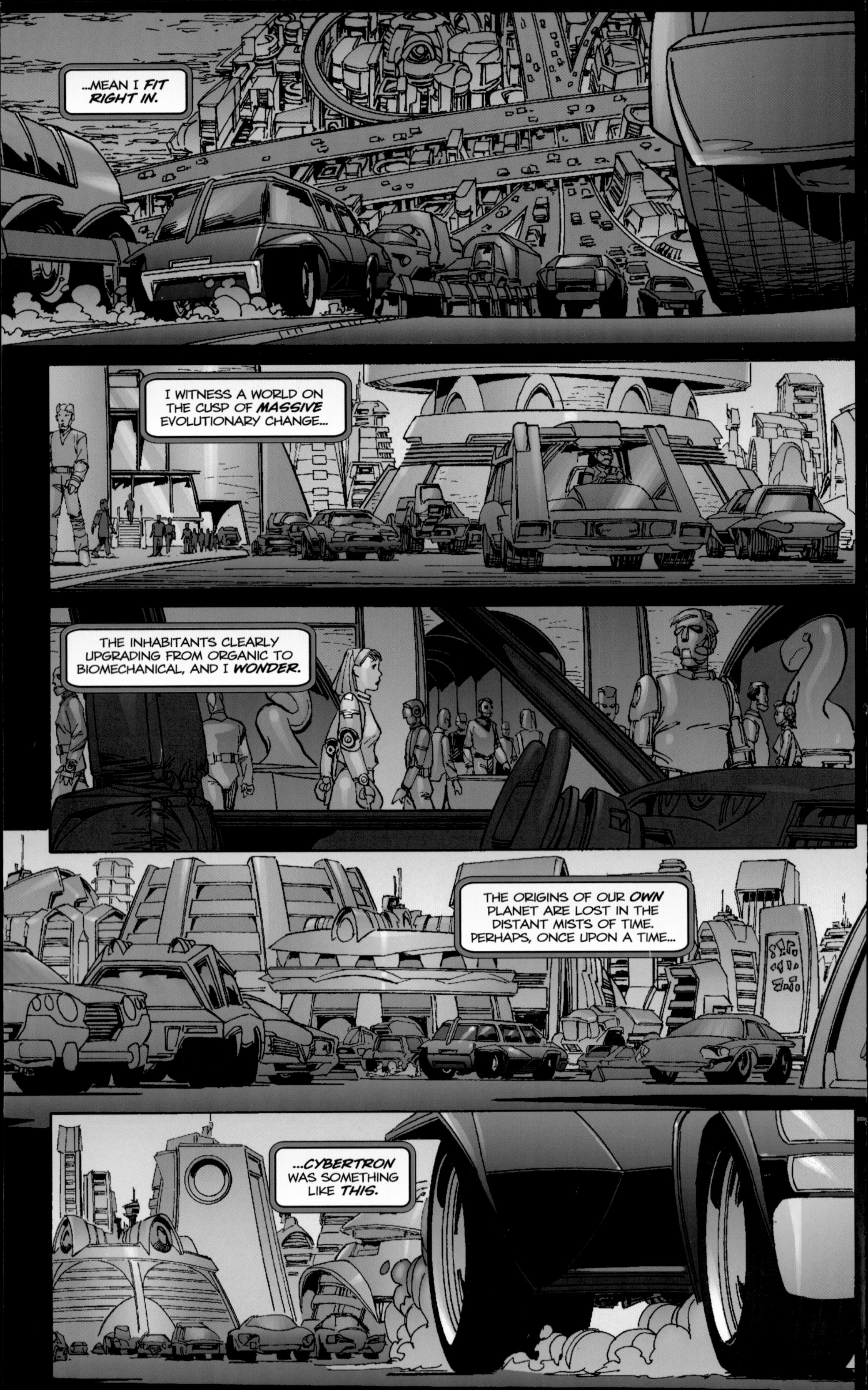
...MEAN I FIT RIGHT IN.
I WITNESS A WORLD ON THE CUSP OF MASSIVE EVOLUTIONARY CHANGE...
THE INHABITANTS CLEARLY UPGRADING FROM ORGANIC TO BIOMECHANICAL, AND I WONDER.
THE ORIGINS OF OUR OWN PLANET ARE LOST IN THE DISTANT MISTS OF TIME. PERHAPS, ONCE UPON A TIME...
...CYBERTRON WAS SOMETHING LIKE THIS.

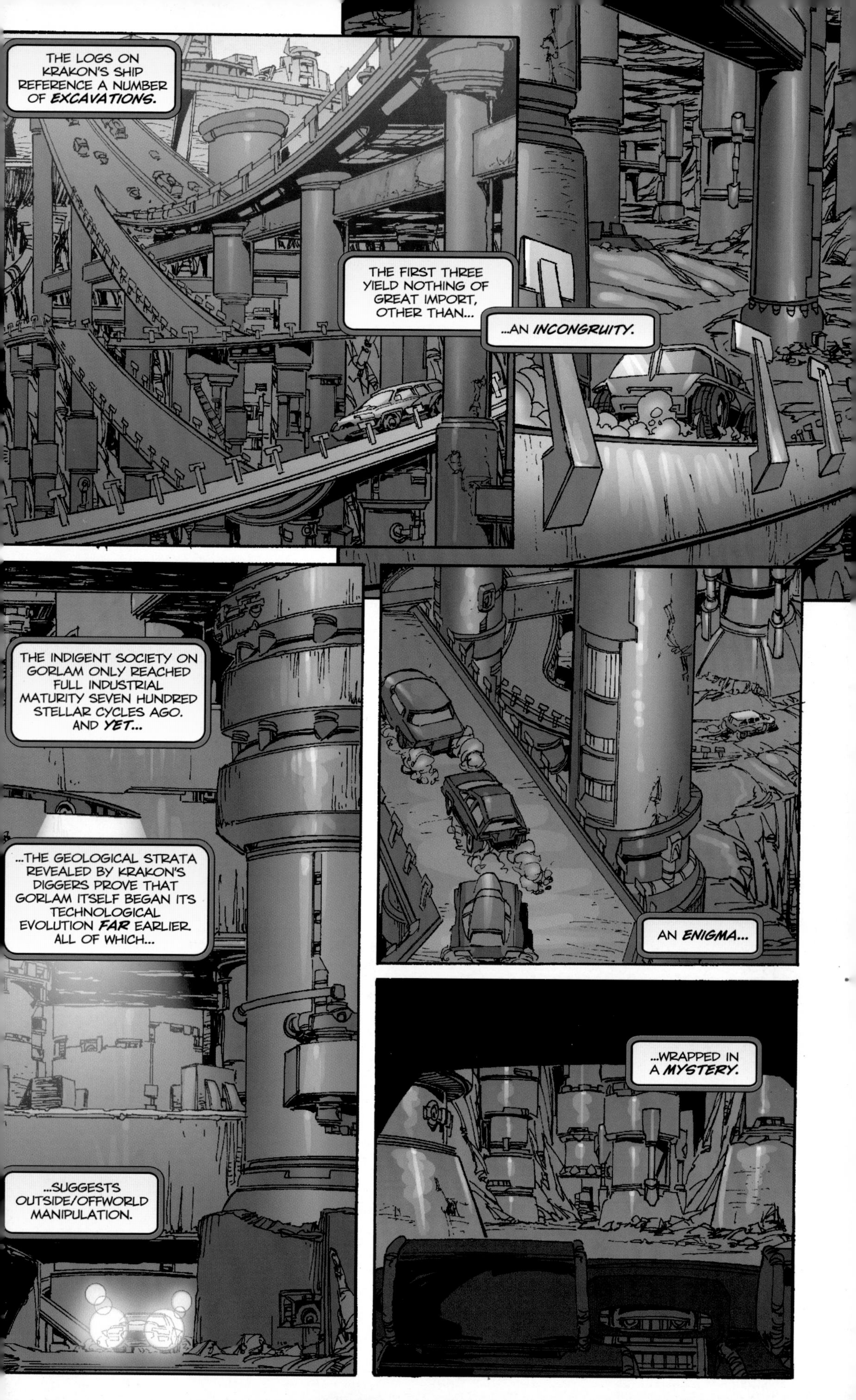
THE LOGS ON KRAKON'S SHIP REFERENCE A NUMBER OF **EXCAVATIONS.**
THE FIRST THREE YIELD NOTHING OF GREAT IMPORT, OTHER THAN...
...AN *INCONGRUITY.*
THE INDIGENT SOCIETY ON GORLAM ONLY REACHED FULL INDUSTRIAL MATURITY SEVEN HUNDRED STELLAR CYCLES AGO. AND *YET*...
...THE GEOLOGICAL STRATA REVEALED BY KRAKON'S DIGGERS PROVE THAT GORLAM ITSELF BEGAN ITS TECHNOLOGICAL EVOLUTION **FAR** EARLIER. ALL OF WHICH...
...SUGGESTS OUTSIDE/OFFWORLD MANIPULATION.
AN *ENIGMA*...
...WRAPPED IN A *MYSTERY.*

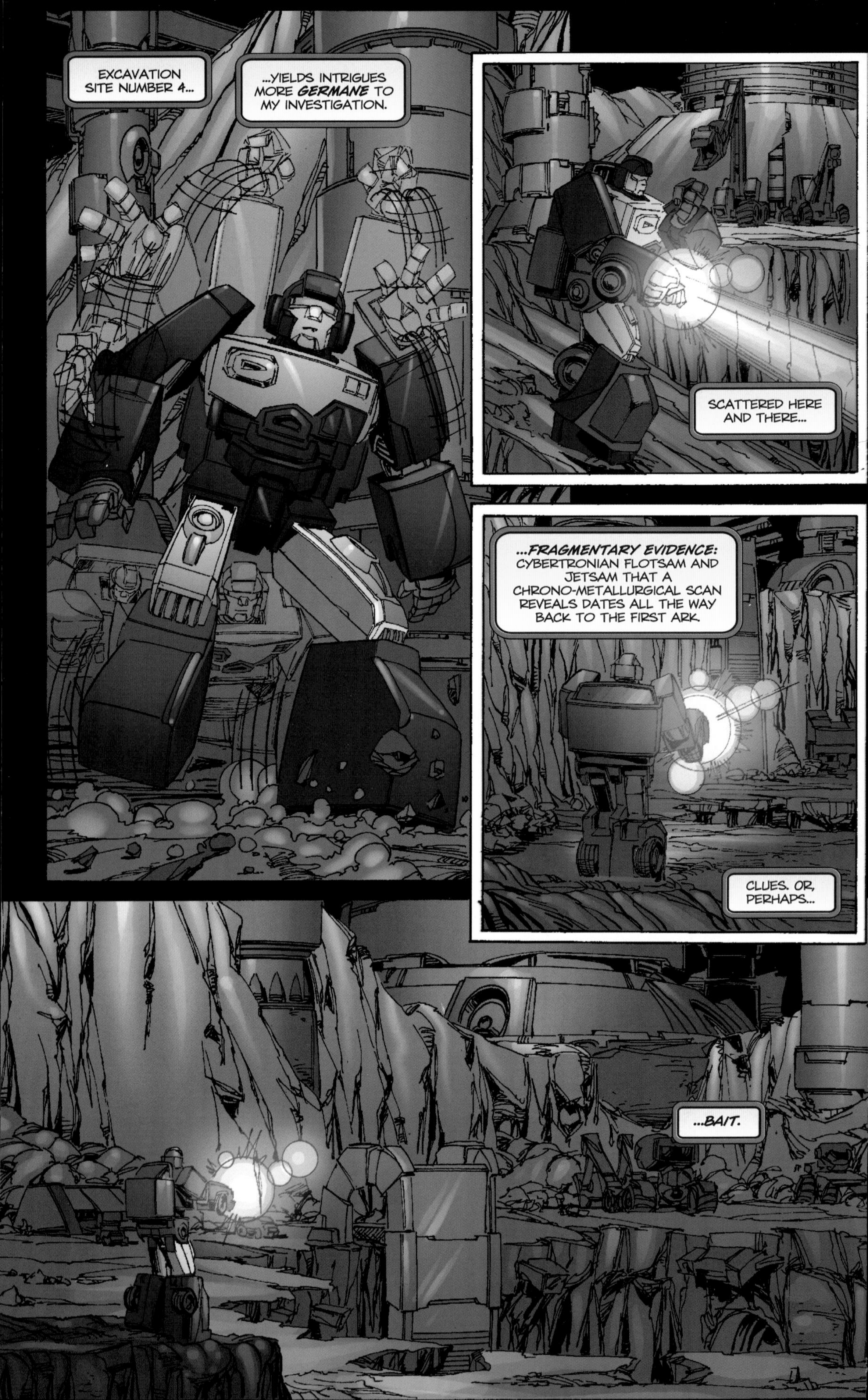
EXCAVATION SITE NUMBER 4...
...YIELDS INTRIGUES MORE GERMANE TO MY INVESTIGATION.
SCATTERED HERE AND THERE...
...FRAGMENTARY EVIDENCE: CYBERTRONIAN FLOTSAM AND JETSAM THAT A CHRONO-METALLURGICAL SCAN REVEALS DATES ALL THE WAY BACK TO THE FIRST ARK.
CLUES. OR, PERHAPS...
...BAIT.

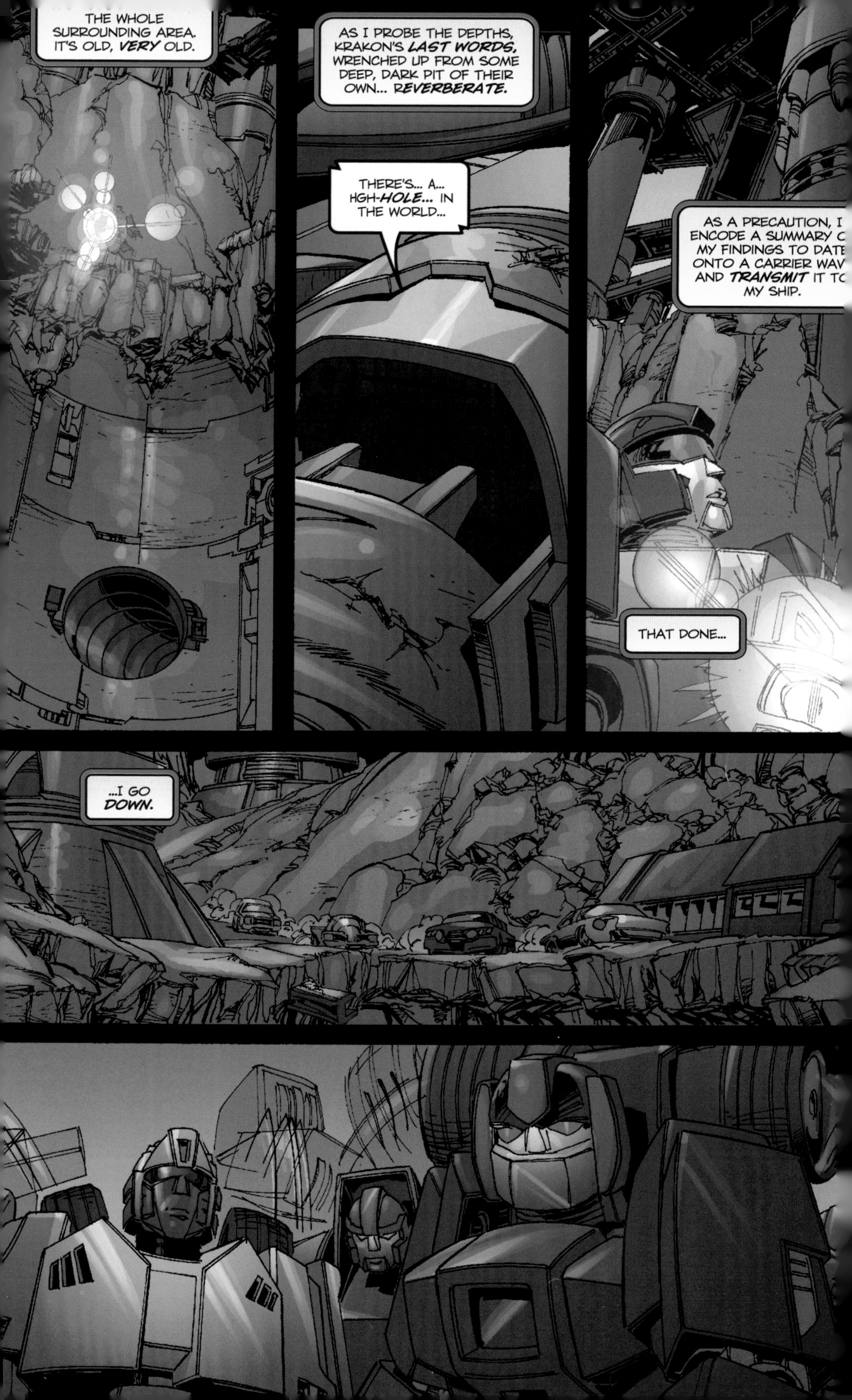
THE WHOLE SURROUNDING AREA. IT'S OLD, VERY OLD.
AS I PROBE THE DEPTHS, KRAKON'S LAST WORDS, WRENCHED UP FROM SOME DEEP, DARK PIT OF THEIR OWN... REVERBERATE.
THERE'S... A... HGH-HOLE... IN THE WORLD...
AS A PRECAUTION, I ENCODE A SUMMARY O MY FINDINGS TO DATE ONTO A CARRIER WAV AND TRANSMIT IT TO MY SHIP.
THAT DONE...
...I GO DOWN.

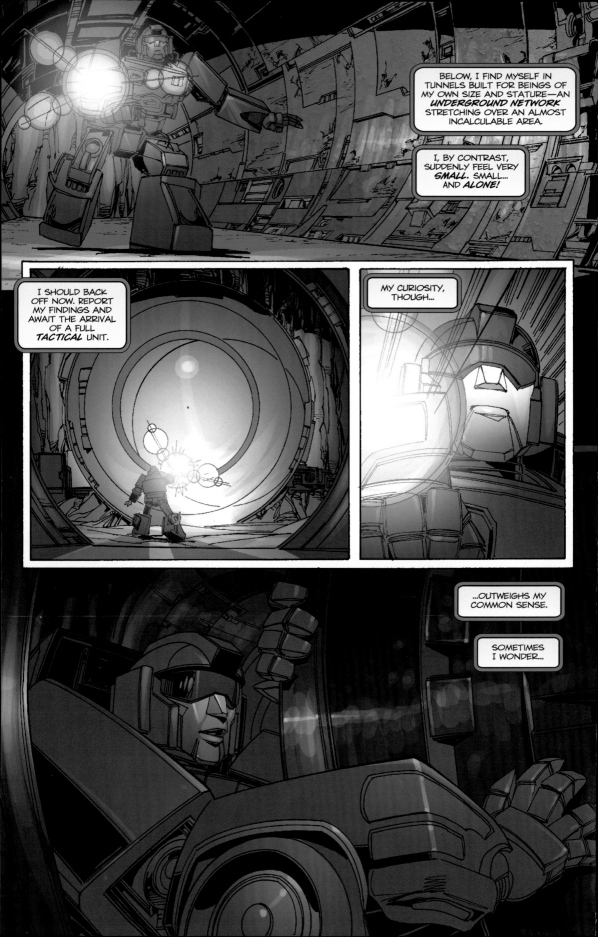

BELOW, I FIND MYSELF IN TUNNELS BUILT FOR BEINGS OF MY OWN SIZE AND STATURE—AN *UNDERGROUND NETWORK* STRETCHING OVER AN ALMOST INCALCULABLE AREA.

I, BY CONTRAST, SUDDENLY FEEL VERY *SMALL*. SMALL.... AND *ALONE!*

I SHOULD BACK OFF NOW. REPORT MY FINDINGS AND AWAIT THE ARRIVAL OF A FULL *TACTICAL* UNIT.

MY CURIOSITY, THOUGH...

...OUTWEIGHS MY COMMON SENSE.

SOMETIMES I WONDER...

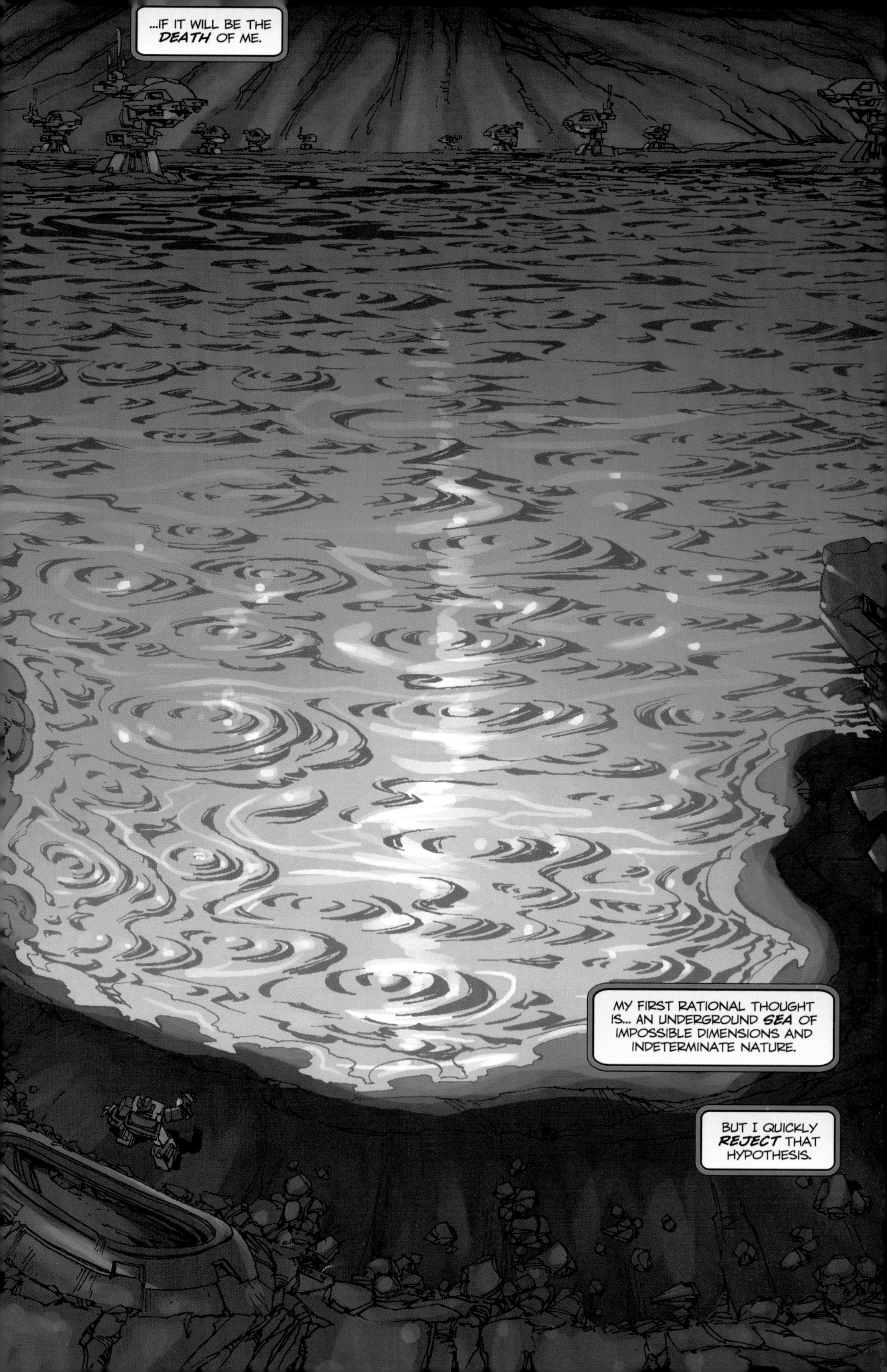
...IF IT WILL BE THE DEATH OF ME.
MY FIRST RATIONAL THOUGHT IS... AN UNDERGROUND SEA OF IMPOSSIBLE DIMENSIONS AND INDETERMINATE NATURE.
BUT I QUICKLY REJECT THAT HYPOTHESIS.

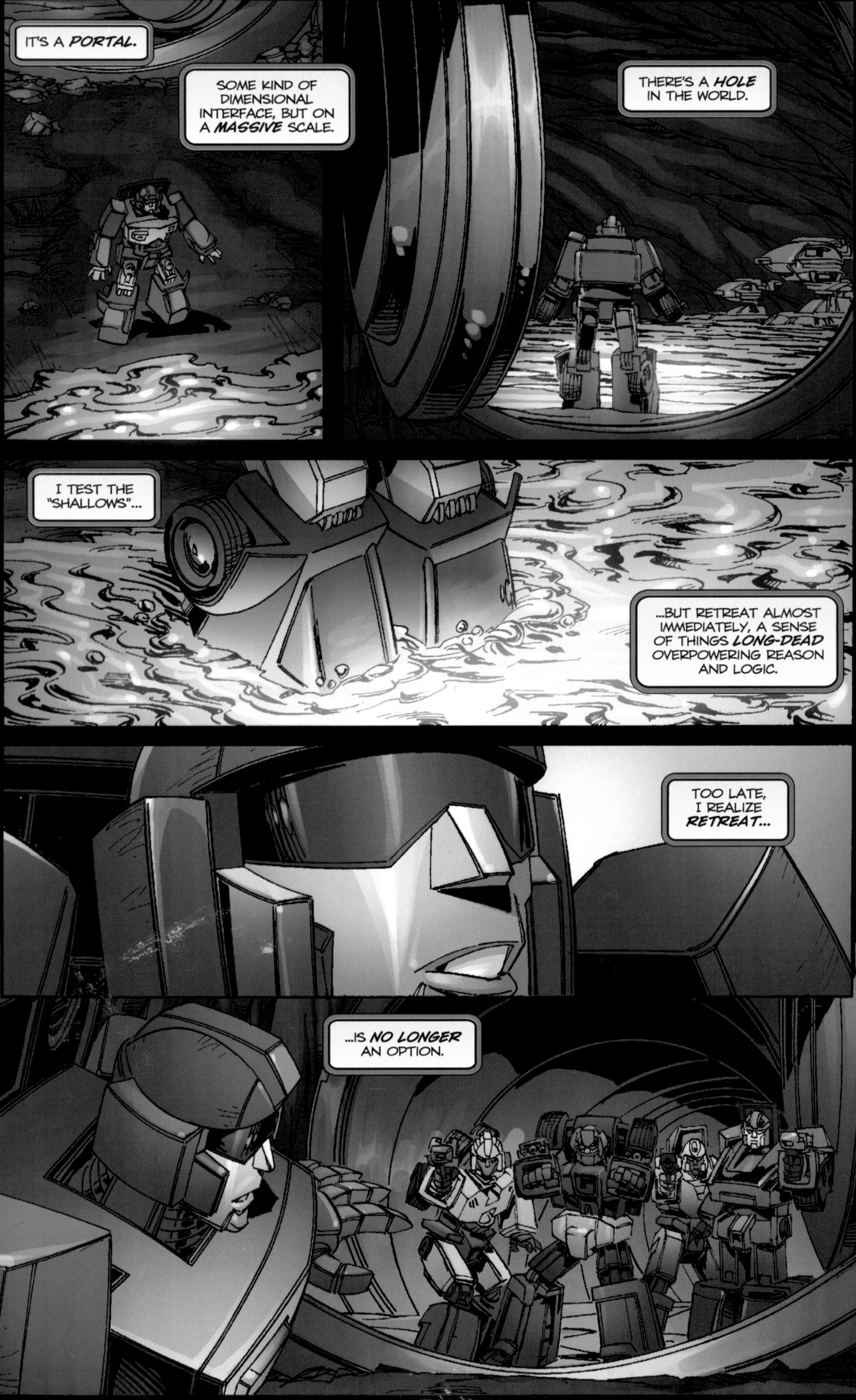
IT'S A PORTAL.
SOME KIND OF DIMENSIONAL INTERFACE, BUT ON A MASSIVE SCALE.
THERE'S A HOLE IN THE WORLD.
I TEST THE "SHALLOWS"...
...BUT RETREAT ALMOST IMMEDIATELY, A SENSE OF THINGS LONG-DEAD OVERPOWERING REASON AND LOGIC.
TOO LATE, I REALIZE RETREAT...
...IS NO LONGER AN OPTION.

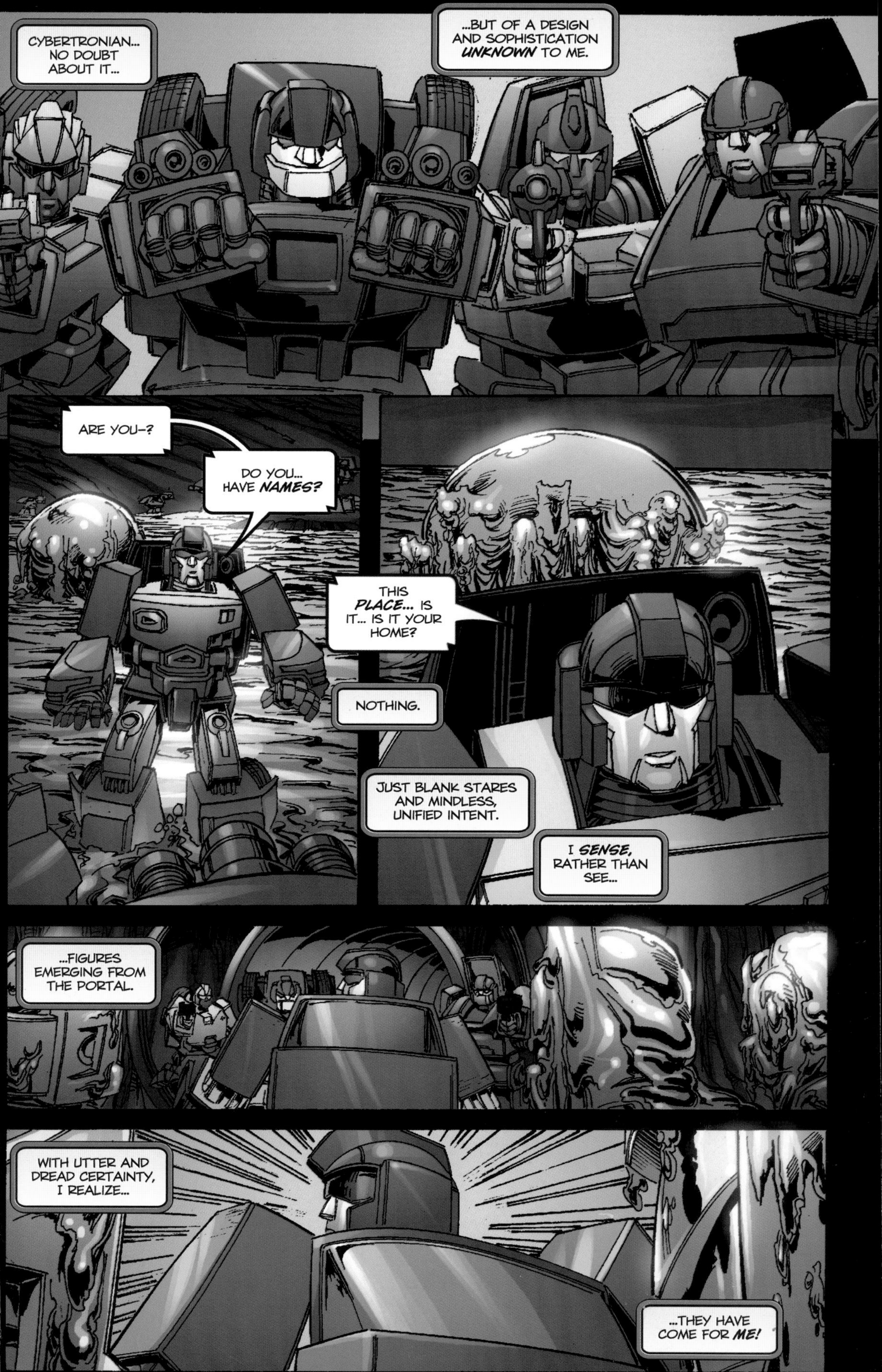
CYBERTRONIAN... NO DOUBT ABOUT IT...
...BUT OF A DESIGN AND SOPHISTICATION UNKNOWN TO ME.
ARE YOU--?
DO YOU... HAVE NAMES?
THIS PLACE... IS IT... IS IT YOUR HOME?
NOTHING.
JUST BLANK STARES AND MINDLESS, UNIFIED INTENT.
I SENSE, RATHER THAN SEE...
...FIGURES EMERGING FROM THE PORTAL.
WITH UTTER AND DREAD CERTAINTY, I REALIZE...
...THEY HAVE COME FOR ME!

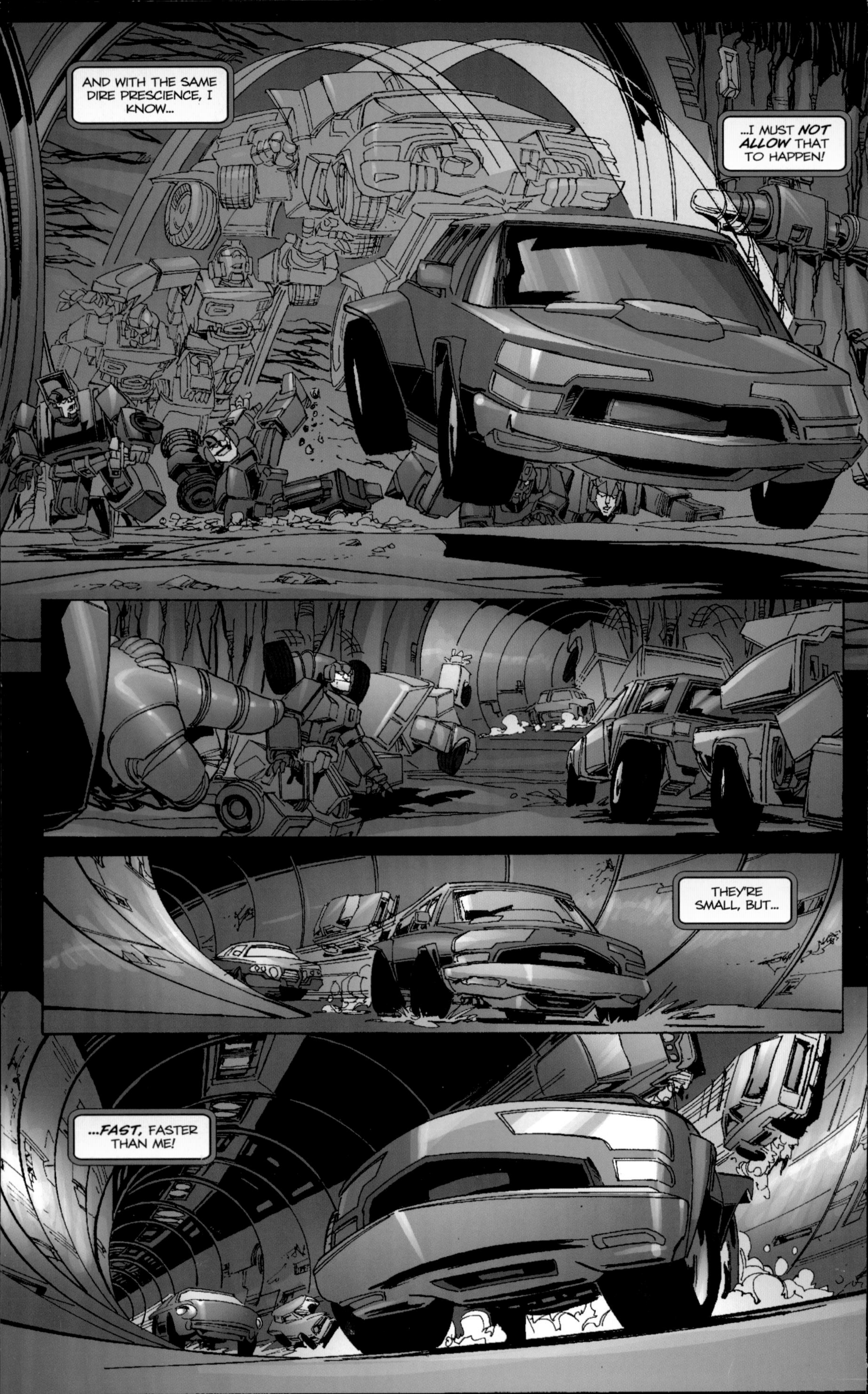
AND WITH THE SAME DIRE PRESCIENCE, I KNOW...
...I MUST NOT ALLOW THAT TO HAPPEN!
THEY'RE SMALL, BUT...
...FAST, FASTER THAN ME!

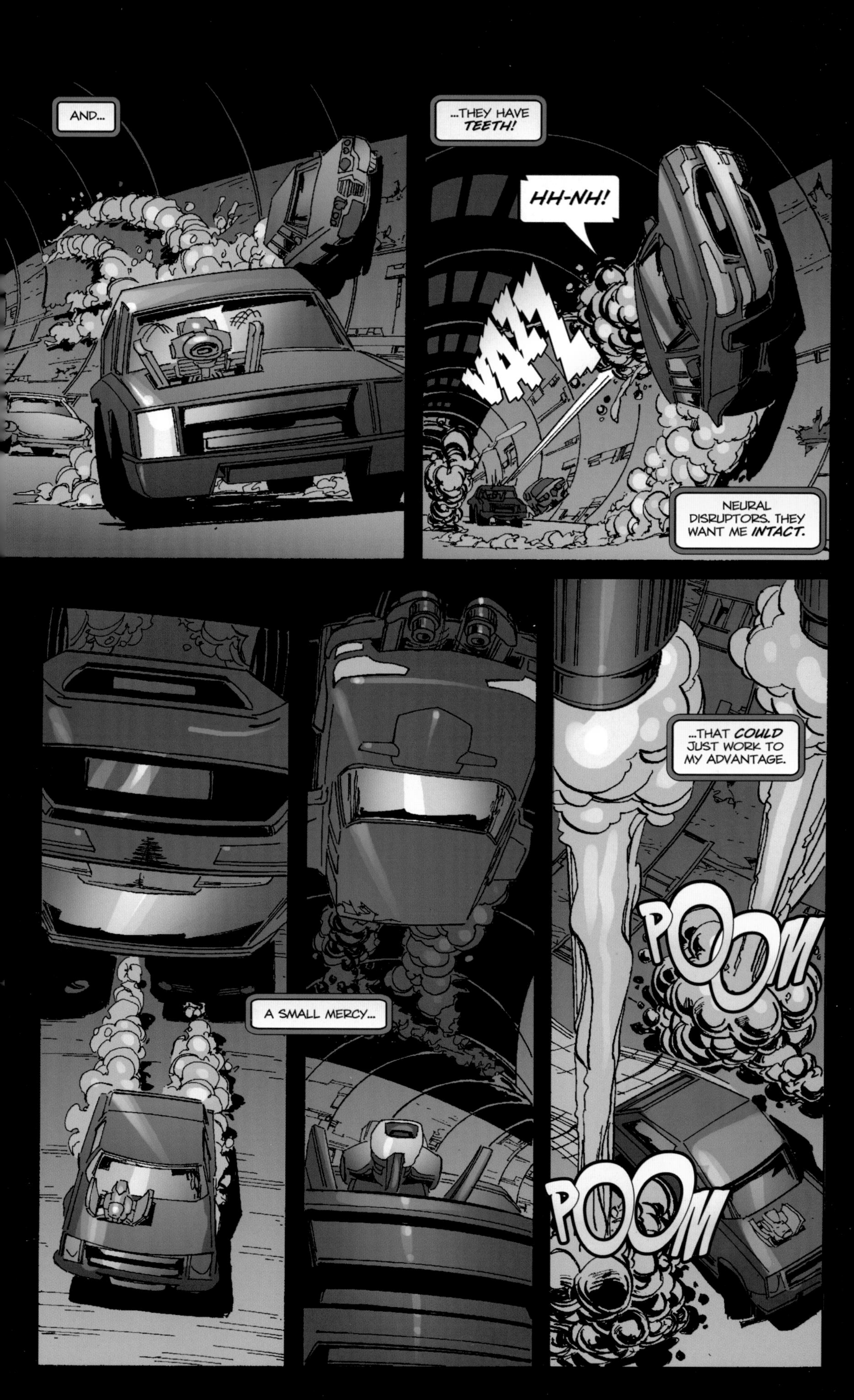

AND...
...THEY HAVE TEETH!
HH-NH!
VAZZ
NEURAL DISRUPTORS. THEY WANT ME INTACT.
A SMALL MERCY...
...THAT COULD JUST WORK TO MY ADVANTAGE.
POOM
POOM

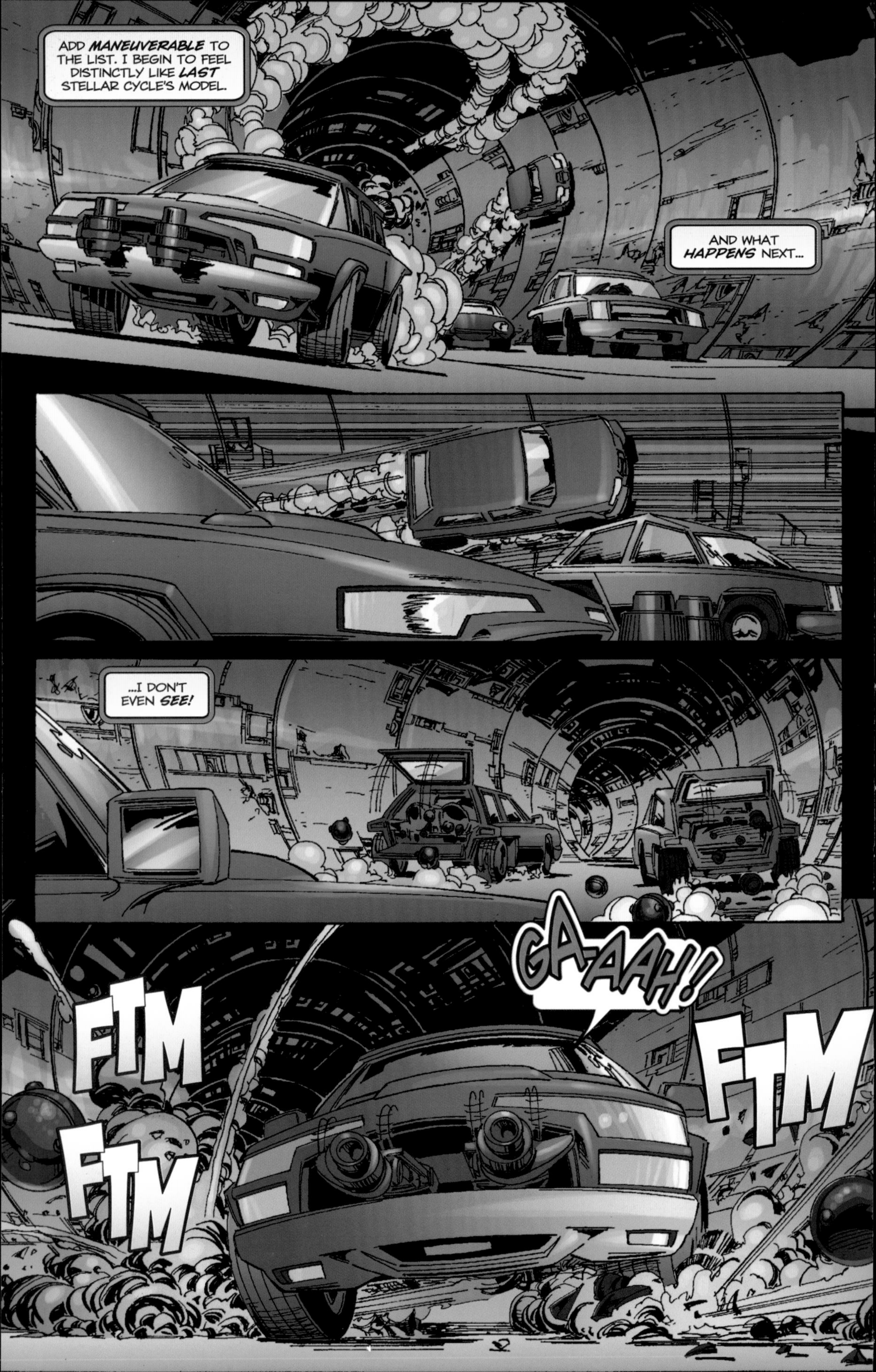
ADD MANEUVERABLE TO THE LIST. I BEGIN TO FEEL DISTINCTLY LIKE LAST STELLAR CYCLE'S MODEL.
AND WHAT HAPPENS NEXT...
...I DON'T EVEN SEE!
GA-AAH!
FTM
FTM
FTM

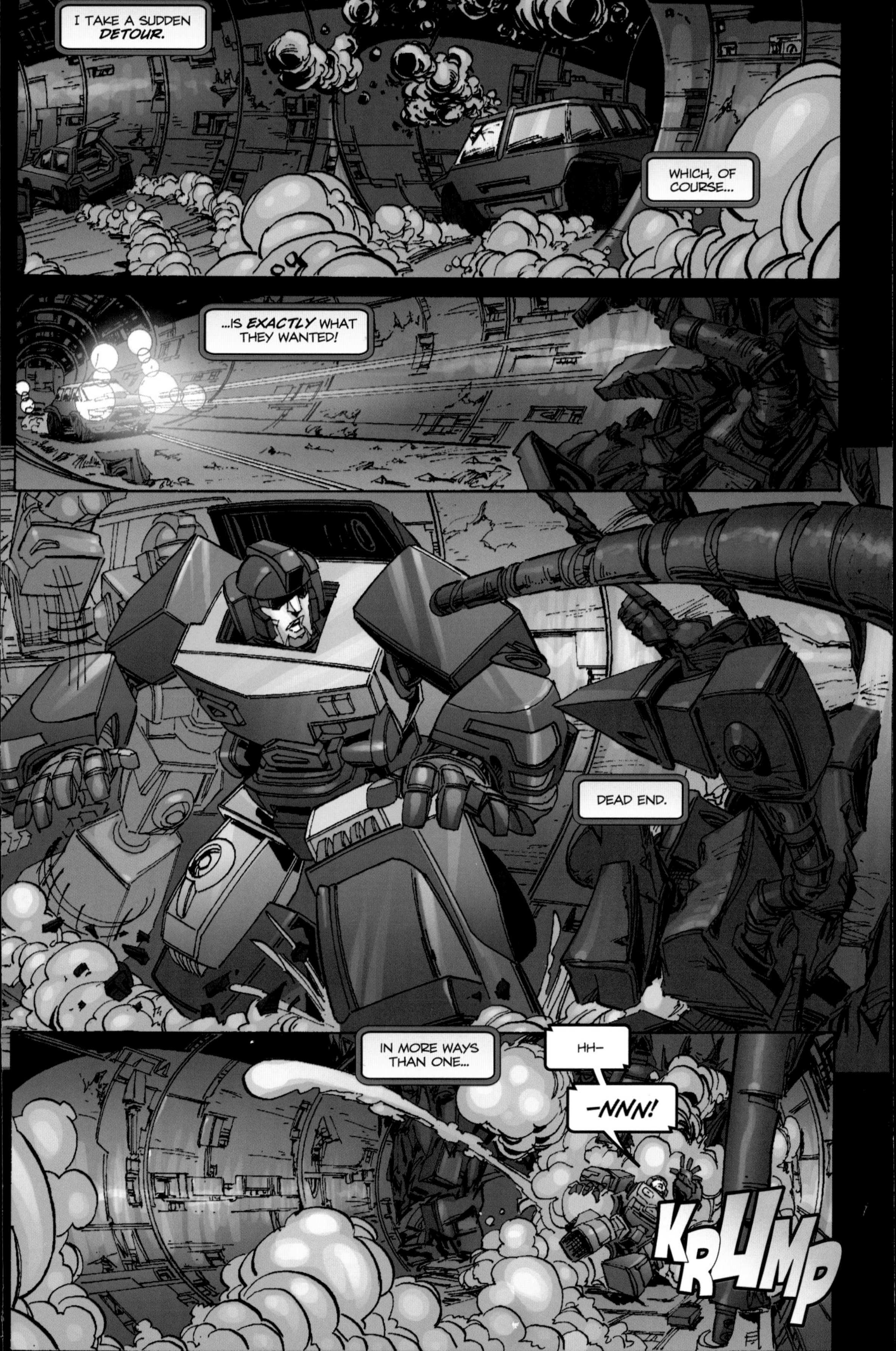
I TAKE A SUDDEN DETOUR.
WHICH, OF COURSE...
...IS EXACTLY WHAT THEY WANTED!
DEAD END.
IN MORE WAYS THAN ONE...
HH-
-NNN!
KRUMP

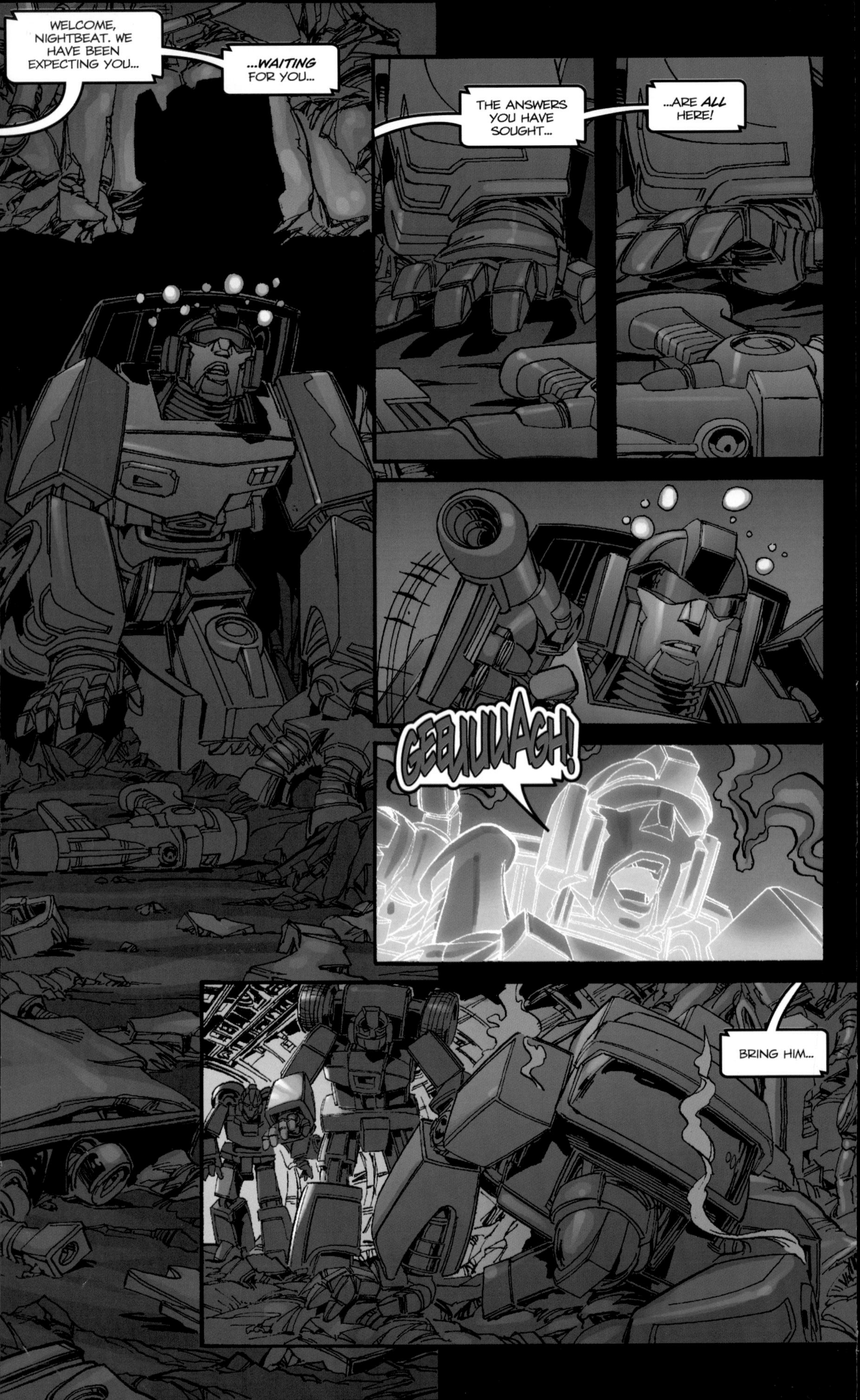
WELCOME, NIGHTBEAT. WE HAVE BEEN EXPECTING YOU...
...*WAITING* FOR YOU...
THE ANSWERS YOU HAVE SOUGHT...
...ARE *ALL* HERE!
GEBUUUAGH!
BRING HIM...

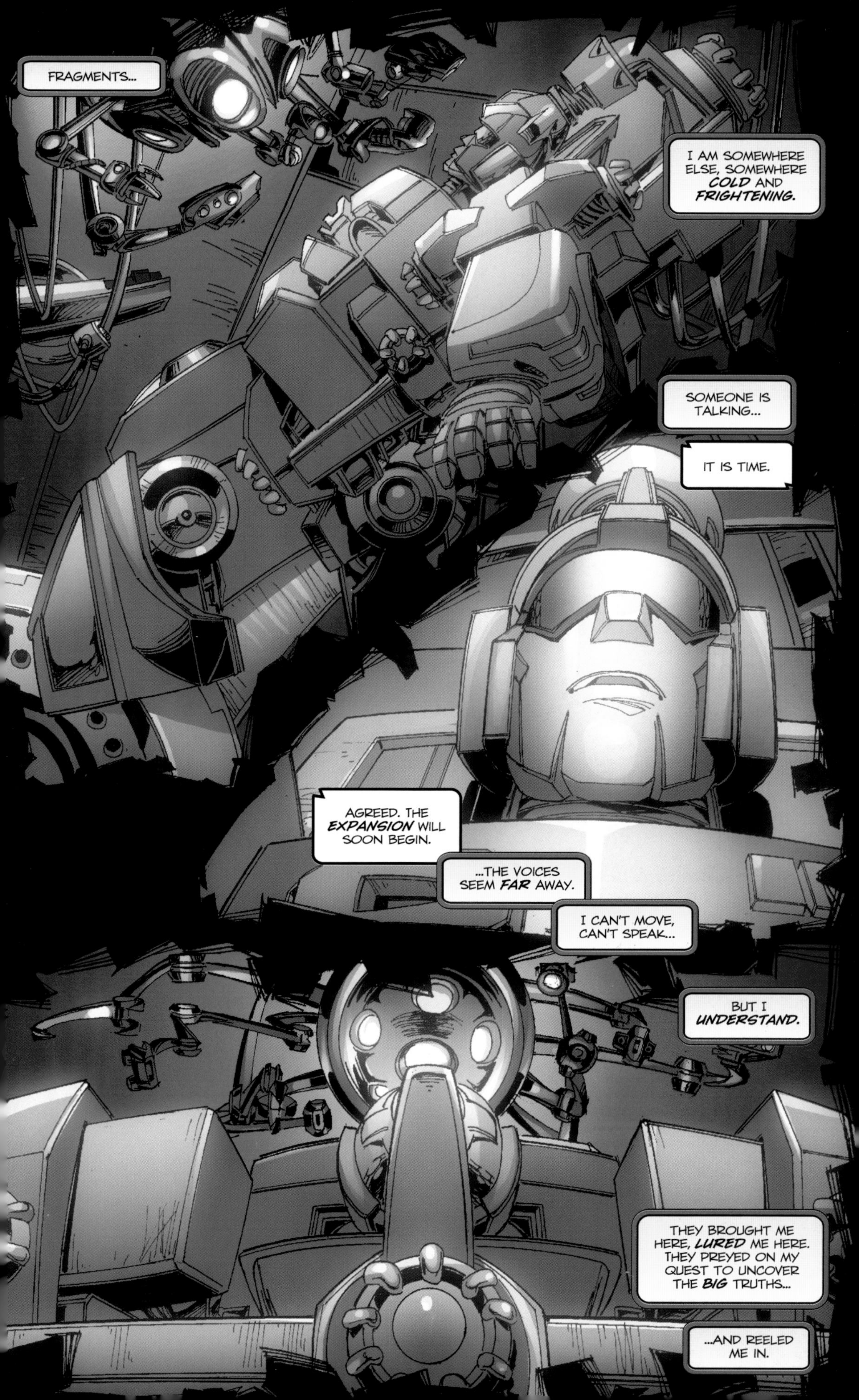
FRAGMENTS...
I AM SOMEWHERE ELSE, SOMEWHERE *COLD* AND *FRIGHTENING.*
SOMEONE IS TALKING...
IT IS TIME.
AGREED. THE *EXPANSION* WILL SOON BEGIN.
...THE VOICES SEEM *FAR* AWAY.
I CAN'T MOVE, CAN'T SPEAK...
BUT I *UNDERSTAND.*
THEY BROUGHT ME HERE, *LURED* ME HERE. THEY PREYED ON MY QUEST TO UNCOVER THE *BIG* TRUTHS...
...AND REELED ME IN.

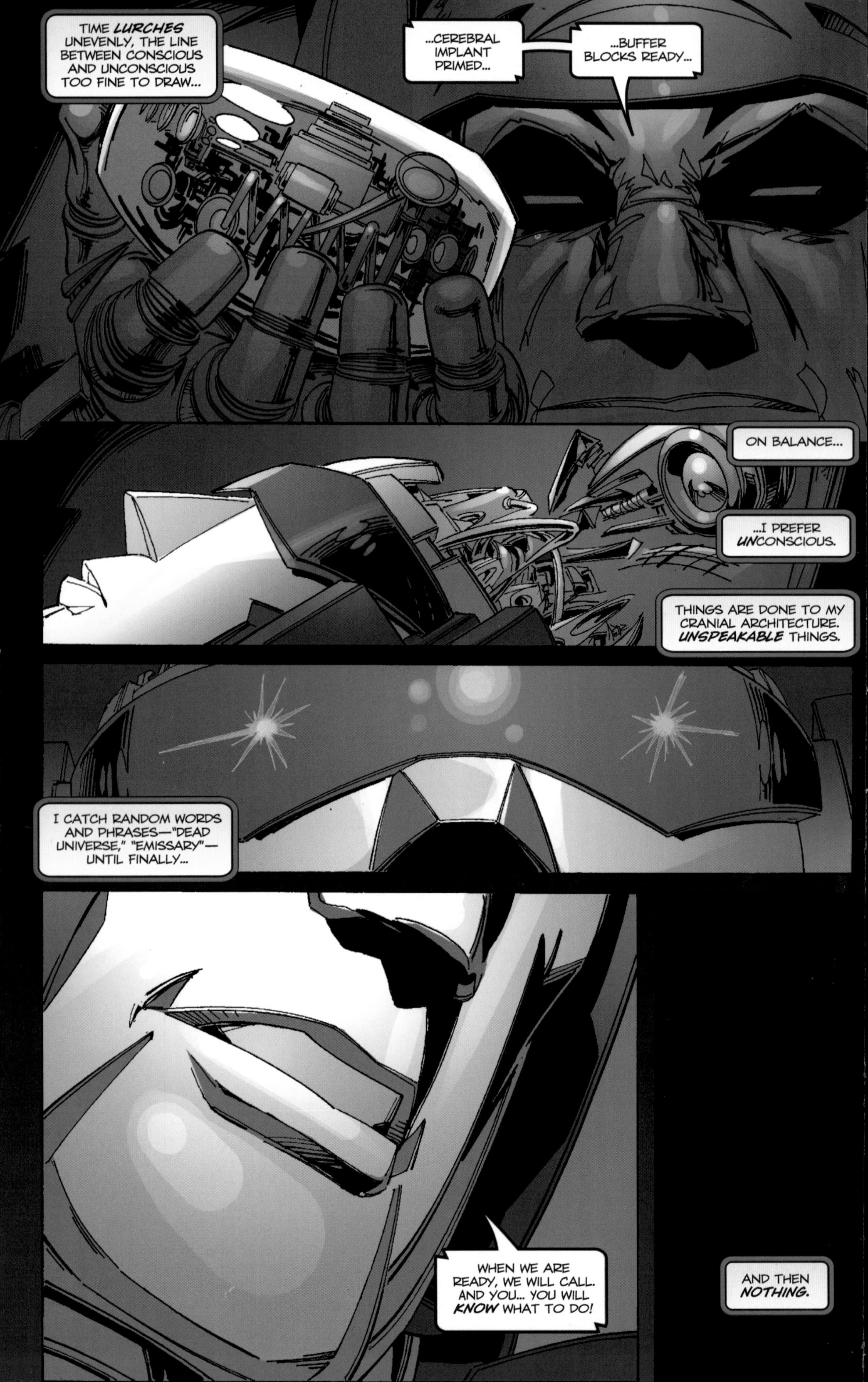
TIME *LURCHES* UNEVENLY, THE LINE BETWEEN CONSCIOUS AND UNCONSCIOUS TOO FINE TO DRAW...
...CEREBRAL IMPLANT PRIMED...
...BUFFER BLOCKS READY...
ON BALANCE...
...I PREFER *UN*CONSCIOUS.
THINGS ARE DONE TO MY CRANIAL ARCHITECTURE. *UNSPEAKABLE* THINGS.
I CATCH RANDOM WORDS AND PHRASES—"DEAD UNIVERSE," "EMISSARY"—UNTIL FINALLY...
WHEN WE ARE READY, WE WILL CALL. AND YOU... YOU WILL *KNOW* WHAT TO DO!
AND THEN *NOTHING.*

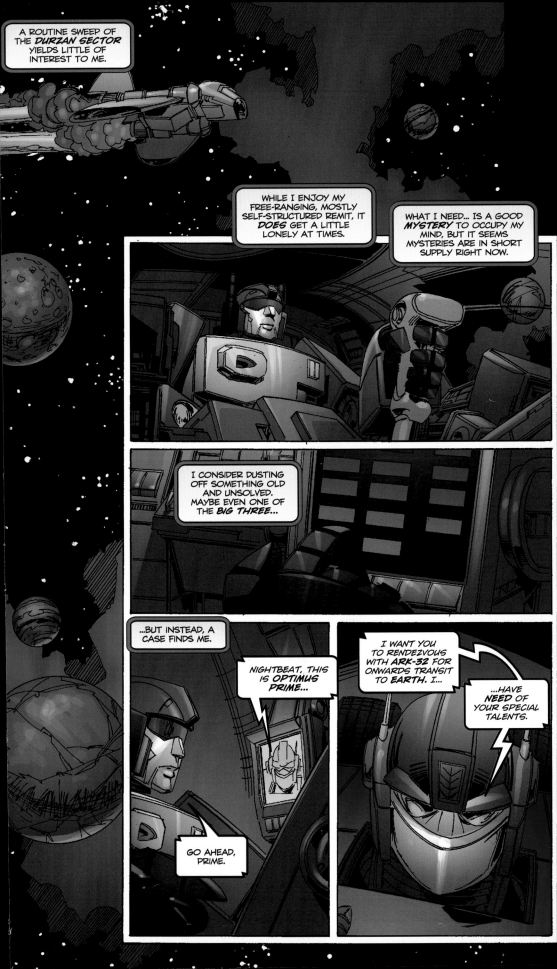

A ROUTINE SWEEP OF THE *DURZAN SECTOR* YIELDS LITTLE OF INTEREST TO ME.

WHILE I ENJOY MY FREE-RANGING, MOSTLY SELF-STRUCTURED REMIT, IT *DOES* GET A LITTLE LONELY AT TIMES.

WHAT I NEED... IS A GOOD *MYSTERY* TO OCCUPY MY MIND, BUT IT SEEMS MYSTERIES ARE IN SHORT SUPPLY RIGHT NOW.

I CONSIDER DUSTING OFF SOMETHING OLD AND UNSOLVED. MAYBE EVEN ONE OF THE *BIG THREE*...

...BUT INSTEAD, A CASE FINDS ME.

NIGHTBEAT, THIS IS *OPTIMUS PRIME*...

GO AHEAD, PRIME.

I WANT YOU TO RENDEZVOUS WITH *ARK-32* FOR ONWARDS TRANSIT TO *EARTH*. I...

...HAVE *NEED* OF YOUR SPECIAL TALENTS.

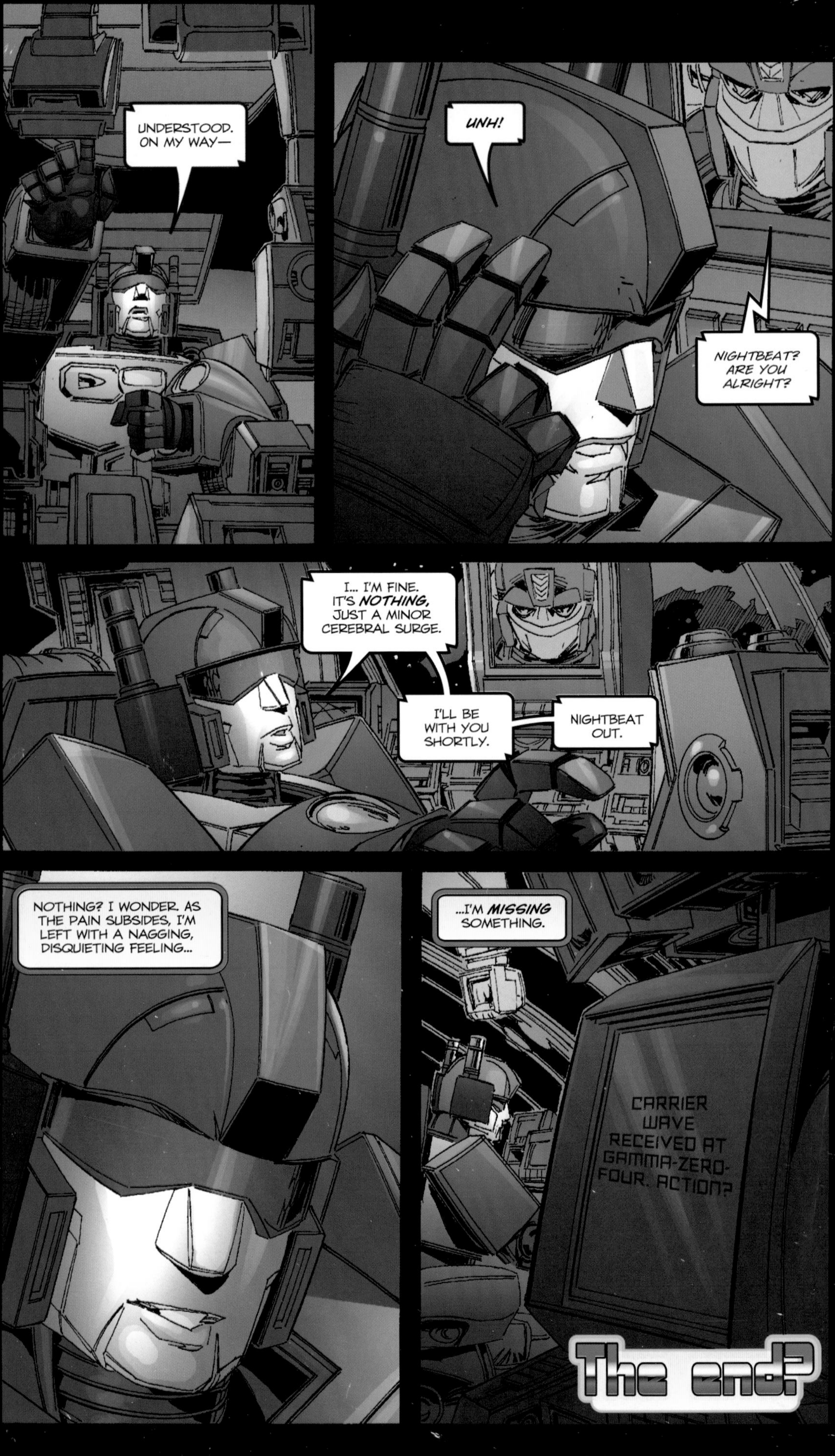
UNDERSTOOD. ON MY WAY—
UNH!
NIGHTBEAT? ARE YOU ALRIGHT?
I... I'M FINE. IT'S *NOTHING*, JUST A MINOR CEREBRAL SURGE.
I'LL BE WITH YOU SHORTLY.
NIGHTBEAT OUT.
NOTHING? I WONDER. AS THE PAIN SUBSIDES, I'M LEFT WITH A NAGGING, DISQUIETING FEELING...
...I'M *MISSING* SOMETHING.
CARRIER WAVE RECEIVED AT GAMMA-ZERO-FOUR. ACTION?
The end?